First edition for the United States, Canada,
Australia and the Philippines published 1988
by Barron's Educational Series, Inc.

First published 1987 by Walker Books, Ltd., London, England

All inquiries should be addressed to:
Barron's Educational Series, Inc.
250 Wireless Boulevard, Hauppauge, NY 11788

Library of Congress Catalog Card No. 87-16779
International Standard Book No. 0-8120-5884-4

Library of Congress Cataloging-in-Publication Data
West, Colin.
Ten little crocodiles.
Summary: Starting with ten little crocodiles clustered
on a bench, the reader counts down from ten to one as a
crocodile is taken away in each picture.
[1. Crocodile—Fiction. 2. Counting] I. Title.
PZ7.W51744Te   1988   [E]   87-16779
ISBN 0-8120-5884-4

Printed in Hong Kong by Dai Nippon (H.K.) Ltd.
789   9685   987654321

Ten Little Crocodiles

Colin West

CHILDRENS PRESS CHOICE

A Barron's title selected for educational distribution

ISBN 0-516-08562-X

Ten little crocodiles
Sitting down to dine,

One of them ate too much pudding,
And then there were…

Nine little crocodiles
Trying to lose weight,

One of them tried till he dropped,
And then there were...

Eight little crocodiles
Who hoped to go to heaven,

One of them went right away,
And then there were…

Seven little crocodiles
Doing magic tricks,

One of them went up in smoke,
And then there were…

Six little crocodiles
Learning how to drive,

One of them drove up a tree,
And then there were...

5

Five little crocodiles
Sailing to the shore,

One of them fell overboard,
And then there were…

Four little crocodiles
Going off to ski,

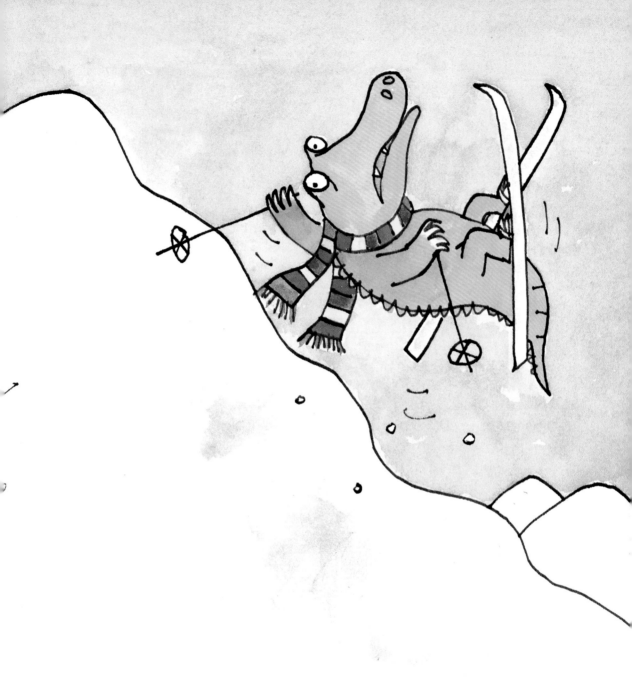

One of them turned somersaults,
And then there were…

Three little crocodiles
Visiting the zoo,

One of them got left behind,
And then there were…

Two little crocodiles
Sitting in the sun,

One of them went home to lunch,
And then there was…

1

One little crocodile
Missing all his friends,

Let's have another look at them
Before the story ends…

One little crocodile
Then gets a big surprise…

All his friends are safe and sound!
He can't believe his eyes!